D1633773

For little John G and his mum ~ *H.O.*
For Wilkie Duncan Morrison ~ *L.S.*

MYRIAD BOOKS LIMITED
35 Bishopsthorpe Road, London SE26 4PA

First published in 2003 by
FRANCES LINCOLN LIMITED
4 Torriano Mews
Torriano Avenue
London NW5 2RZ

ISBN 1 84746 046 1
EAN 9 781 84746 046 2

Printed in China

The Best Party Of Them All

HIAWYN ORAM

Illustrated by LUCY SU

MYRIAD BOOKS LIMITED

Katie and Harry were twins.
They wanted it to be their birthday.

They wished and wished it was,
but it wasn't.

It was their friend Tim's birthday.
This was the invitation to his party.

You are invited to a **Dinosaur Party!**

Date: Saturday

Time: 11.30 – 2.00pm

Dress: Jurassic Park Place: The Museum

Food: pine-needle burgers, fir-cone fries, swamp jelly

"We want a Dinosaur Party when it's our birthday," said Harry.

"With pine-needle burgers and swamp jelly," said Katie.

Then they dressed up...

and went to the party and forgot it wasn't
their birthday because they had such a...

megasauric time.

But when the next invitation came
it still wasn't their birthday.
It was Mary's.

Please come
to my party
It's going to be
a
Circus
Date: Sunday
Time: 2.00p.m.
Place: My house
Dress: for the
Big Top

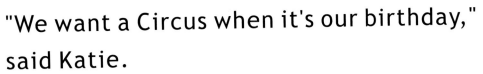

"We want a Circus when it's our birthday,"
said Katie.
   "With a Big Top and Tickle the Clown,"
said Harry.
Then they dressed up...

and went to the party and forgot it wasn't
their birthday because they had such a...

Silly time.

But when the next invitation came
it still wasn't their birthday.
It was Nicola's.

To: Katie and Harry
It's my Birthday
& you are invited
to a
Picnic in the Park

On: Friday at 1.00p.m.
At: The Ponds in the Park
Dress: Woodland Creatures
Food: Ant sandwiches, ladybird cakes, squashed wasp biscuits

"When it's our birthday, we want
a Picnic in the Park," said Harry.
"With Ant sandwiches and Ladybird
cakes, but NO wasps," said Katie.
Then they dressed up...

and went to the party and forgot it wasn't
their birthday because they had such a...

wonderfully wild time.

But when the next invitation came
it STILL wasn't their birthday.
It was Halloween and George
was having a party.

You are invited to a
HALLOWEEN PARTY
Date: Saturday   Time: After dark!
Place: bottom of the   Food: Pumpkin soup,
garden!   Dracula cake!
Parents: welcome   Dress: witches, ghosts
(with magic spells)   black cats
Going Home Presents:
spelling books!

"When it's our birthday we want
a Halloween Party," said Harry.
"With pumpkins and witches even
if it's not Halloween," said Katie.
Then they dressed up...

and went to the party and forgot it wasn't
their birthday because they had such a...

whoOO... scary time!

But when the NEXT invitation came...
there were ten of them and they
were BLANK.

"Now," said their mum, "what do you think these are for?"

"OUR PARTY!" cried the Twins.
"Hurry, write in OUR PARTY!"

So their mum wrote...

You are invited to
THE TWINS' PARTY
On Friday at 2 o'clock
at 4 Rockery Drive

And when the day came, they were
so excited they could hardly dress

because it wasn't a Dinosaur Party, it wasn't
a Circus Party, it wasn't a Picnic Party,
it wasn't a Halloween Party...

wilder than **wonderfully wild**

scarier than just
whoOO... scary

and for Katie and Harry it was easily...

THE BEST PARTY OF THEM ALL!